"When he touched you, did you yearn for him like you yearn for me?"

She barely took one step before she found herself in Grant's arms, his lips crushing hers in a bruising kiss. Although she should have been outraged, a small part of her was just relieved to feel him against her.

"When he kissed your lips did he make you feel like this?"

"Grant don't. Please stop. Not like this, not in anger. Please." Even as the words left her lips her body was betraying her. He lifted up her skirt and without hesitation inserted his chunky finger in her wet sheet. Amanda's legs buckled.

"When he fucked you did you juice as much as you are juicing for me?" Grant words were laced with torment.

"Please stop," Amanda groaned.

"Did you tell HIM to stop or were you enjoying yourself too much?" *How did you not know you were mine?*

"I…I can't change anything that happened. And I can't deny that he didn't force himself on me. But that was before – before I knew," she whimpered.

Her words nearly shattered him. He knew what it was like to fill her, to stretch her. He knew what it was like to have her ride him, slick with hot heat, and he resented that any other man before or since him had ever made a claim on her. It was irrational, unfair but her pleading voice could not assuage his anger… his shame.

BOOKS BY MONTANA NIGHT

BILLIONAIRE BROTHERS: HAMILTON

The Russian Mail-Order Bride
The Stand-In Bride
The Tycoon's Replacement Bride Part 1
The Tycoon's Replacement Bride Part 2
The Tycoon's Replacement Bride Part 3

Author website:

montananight.labelleauboisdormant.co.uk

THE
TYCOON'S

Replacement Bride (3)

[Billionaire Romance: BBW]

MONTANA NIGHT

For queries, comments or feedback please contact La Belle Au Bois Dormant Publishing.

www.labelleauboisdormant.co.uk
info@labelleauboisdormant.co.uk

Printed in the United Kingdom

ISBN-13: 978-1-909916-40-1

ACKNOWLEDGMENTS

To my husband, because *he is the wind beneath my wings.* To my mother because without her I would never have been. To my friends because their encouragement was invaluable. To my readers for loving my books. To you all I say thank you.

Montana Night

PREVIOUSLY (PART 1)

Amanda Cardwell's best friend arranged to be a mail-order bride for Billionaire Tycoon Grant Hamilton, but she backs out last minute. So Amanda steps in to save the day. After all, one look at her curvy self and the billionaire will cancel the marriage contract and that will be that. At least that was the plan. But she didn't count on the sex-factor.

A fake replacement mail-order bride mix-up turns into a very real engagement, with a real man. But the path of love is never a smooth one and Amanda is just about to learn how true that is.

PREVIOUSLY (PART 2)

Sheikh Samir Ben Alid, billionaire playboy had never seen such an exquisite sight as the fiery voluptuous beauty. He hasn't met a girl who can resist him, and Amanda is just one challenge he cannot do without. Luckily enough for the sheikh she can't remember her name and she couldn't tell you who Grant Hamilton is.

Secluded in a heady world of sex and dominance Amanda's self-restraint is sorely tested as her desire for the bad boy sheikh is kindled.

CHAPTER 1

Billionaire Tycoon Grant Hamilton, leaned forward against the barrel of his assault gun, and assessed the developing situation with narrow eyes. After scouring the world in search for his kidnapped fiancée, Amanda Cardwell, the moment had finally come to retrieve her from the clutches of her kidnapper. Based on information from Bahrain, Amanda was being held captive by Sheikh Samir Ben Alid, in the desert harem he was currently gazing at.

The Sheikh's secluded estate was built around an unbelievably beautiful oasis. It sprawled over an area extending further than 20 miles. The shade of the trees nearest the pool served as a resting place, created around stunning, lush gardens.

In terms of any real fortress like protection, it had none. Whilst the gardens and trees created seclusion and intimacy, they also obscured any view of approaching enemies.

Currently, a pair of six-man teams were scattered around the parameter awaiting Grant's orders. The men had been instructed to only shoot to kill if they absolutely had to. Hopefully, this rescue would never come to that.

More comfortable in the boardroom than on a mission that involved storming a guarded desert harem, Grant would not have been anywhere else than at the forefront of this assault. Snapping out of his musing he glanced up and noted the approaching dark, swirling clouds, moving steadily in their direction.

"I think luck is about to be our lady tonight."

"Really?" his brother Alexander replied, moving forward to get into a better position to cover the estate.

"Yes, it's another four hours until sundown, but with the overhanging clouds we will be able to execute the rescue plan in the next 20 minutes."

"I know you want to get to her as quickly as possible but I still think we need to give Tatianna more time inside the harem to locate her."

"We are going in as soon as the sky is overcast." Grant replied, his voice cold and uncompromising.

Alex took a deep breath. Although he worked for Uncle Sam as a spy and a sniper, he had relinquished control of the rescue operation from the onset to his brother. No one could argue with Grant when he had made his mind up. He was in his Louis VII mood as their mother called it. Still, he had to try.

"You are making this personal," he commented with a frown.

Grant continued to look at the dark mass emerging in the sky overhead, a dark storm to mirror the anger coursing through his veins. He remembered the blood on the note left for him. Emotions that had been bottled up since the kidnapping, started rising to the surface. Determined he stomped them down. He turned and looked at his brother.

"Samir Ben Alid made this personal when he abducted Amanda. I am not going to pretend. I want to wring the living daylights out of him, and pummel him to a pulp." His gaze reverted to the estate.

Alex sighed inwardly and thanked God he had better control of his emotions. "Be that as it may, this all seems a bit too easy," he replied. "I can't imagine that we've gotten this far and haven't set off any hidden alarms."

"What the hell are you trying to say?" Grant retorted, without removing his observation for one second, from the sprawling oasis estate.

"I don't know. I have a bad feeling," Alex replied, giving his brother a humorless smile.

Grant rubbed his temples, eyes still firmly fixed on the target. "I know what you mean. The trail from Bahrain that led us straight to Samir's door step seemed a bit too easy."

"Perhaps we should pull back, regroup, and negotiate Ben Alid's surrender," Alex suggested.

Grant shook his head. "It's not like you to be this apprehensive. I thought you were the big shot, super spy?"

"Well, I used to not give a damn," Alex said. "Now I've got a wife who at this very moment is infiltrating an enemy camp without me at her back."

"You are lucky Tati isn't here to hear you say any of this. She would kick your uptight behind."

"She would definitely try," Alex muttered and they both burst out laughing.

When Grant had met his new sister in-law, a couple of days earlier, a misplaced comment had her flipping him over on his ass. Tatianna Romanovsky Hamilton was an ex Russian Internal Security Agent. She looked like a curvaceous bombshell, but was deadly as hell. He was not about to underestimate her, or her skills again.

For two days, they had been waiting for the perfect opportunity for Tatianna to infiltrate the harem. When pictures had been taken of Samir and Amanda running around like two lovebirds Grant had almost ordered the men to storm the place. But the nerves of steel that served him well in the boardroom had ensured he stuck to the original plan.

It was well known in the area that Ben Alid was planning an opulent party and feast in the coming days. This meant a lot of unknown people walking into and out of the oasis estate. Despite the almost non-existing security, a stealth approach was the most prudent strategy. Tati had slipped in completely un-noticed, covered from head to toe, pretending to be part of the catering team. *Infiltration, extraction,* and hopefully *zero loss of life.*

Grant mulled over the risks of the operation as he looked through the scope of his AK47 rifle. Through the window of the east wing of the estate, a young woman was dancing. Her movements showed passion and joy. She was surrounded by other women, who were watching and clapping in encouragement. Yes, the risks were clear and present. If anything went horribly wrong not only Amanda, but also these innocent women might get hurt.

A tremor went through his body and for a split second, rage flowed, hot and pure, unmasked by his usual business veneer.

Those who knew the Hamilton brothers always assumed that Grant was the calm, cool, collected one. Only Alex and Chase knew that sometimes, that veneer cracked, and the rage that poured out was lethal.

One day in middle school some older, rich punk had beaten up Chase and stolen his Sony Walkman. Grant had found Alex holding their younger, bloodied brother. Although he had no clear memory of what happened next, apparently he had made them take him to the boy, and given him such a bad beating it required three people to get him off of the poor student. The boy had ended up spending a week in the hospital and Grant had almost been thrown out of the boarding school. Luckily enough, Hamilton money had ensured that hadn't happened.

Ever since that day, Grant's emotions were always kept in check. He did not do anything on impulse. That was until he had set his eyes on Amanda Cardwell.

Although he didn't believe in love at first sight, now in retrospect he realized that was exactly what had happened. She had stolen his heart with one smile. The knowledge that he had put her in danger ate away at him, the demon of rage riding him hard.

Suddenly a figure emerged from the east corner of the grounds. It was Tatianna Hamilton, and she had Amanda in tow. They were making a run for it to the far end of the estate where the Sheikh kept his prized vehicles. Hot on their trail were men dressed in black from head to toe.

Men that did not belong to the harem's guard team, and shouldn't have been there at all. Somehow, something else was afoot, beside the covert rescue operation. Grant frowned. The men were gaining on the women.

He squeezed the trigger of his rifle and one of the men fell with a heavy thud. Even as Grant took the shot, Alex's gun went off simultaneously, and the second henchman fell.

Grant dropped his assault weapon, whipped out his pistol and started running. "I am going in," he shouted over his shoulder to his brother.

"I am right behind you," Alex responded grabbing his own handgun, and launched into a full sprint. *All units, stand firm, cover Grant and I,* he instructed over his handheld military radio.

As Grant ran, he knew he was being rash. Better men were at hand for this, but he zig zagged his way down to the estate anyway, trusting Alex and the team to keep the guards and any snipers off of him.

A gunshot rang out. A bullet whizzed past Grant's right shoulder chipping off the bark of a tree he had just veered past.

Heedless of the danger, he continued his sprint.

CHAPTER 2

S heikh Samir Ben Alid, had four dozen concubines, and frequented some of the most eclectic, bondage dungeons in Europe. He was almost thirty-six, and ruthless in the board room. Ruthless, with everything. Samir Ben Alid did not fall in love. Or at least he thought he didn't. But the anguish he was feeling, at the thought of ever giving up Amanda Cardwell, had to be love.

After their tryst, which lasted through to the early morning, he had been unable to sleep, his mind mulling over the day's events. Amanda had been out like a light, the coupling proving too exhausting for her. As he watched her sleep he was tormented by insecurities.

He wasn't used to worrying about anything. Much less what a woman did, said, or thought. Nevertheless, the knowledge that her memories could separate them left him in an unusual state of anxiety. When had it all changed? When had he decided to keep his flame-haired beauty to himself? As he mused over these questions, he concluded that it did not matter. Ultimately, the memory of her response to his demanding desires, was proof enough that he could still make her his, mind, body and soul. *And mine she shall be.*

Suddenly the revenge he had been after seemed insignificant. Amanda Cardwell was his, and he had no intention of letting her go. He knew she would be disappointed that the freedom he had promised her was not forthcoming. But why would she want to be free after what they had just experienced? There was so much more to explore.

He had not yet completely tamed the defiant flame that burned within her. As much as he thought he loved her, the fantasy he was entertaining, of her complete submission, was even now arousing his manhood. His passions grew darker in tandem with the hardening of his cock. Accustomed to owning and acquiring anything and everything, Samir looked at the opulence that surrounded him, and decide no woman in her right mind would refuse what he had to offer. His mind finally at peace, he decided Amanda might enjoy waking up to his hard possession. The image in his mind made him smile. It was time to wake up his sleeping beauty.

His cell phone rang, shaking him out of his musing. He looked at it, curiosity aroused. Few people had the number to this particular cell, and rare were the occasions it actually rang. With a frown he picked it up and noticed, the callers' number was blocked.

"Hello."

"Samir." The voice was metallic, clearly modified through a digital voice enhancer, but Samir recognized it instantly. It was a voice he had hoped never to hear again.

"What do you want?" he replied.

"Is that anyway to speak to the person, who provided you with the means to get back at the Hamilton's?"

"As I remember, you were compensated handsomely for your 'help,'" Samir responded, steel in his voice. Blinded by his need for revenge he had not questioned the motives, or scruples of the man who had provided him with the means to kidnap Grant Hamilton's bride-to-be.

"Tsk, tsk. Aren't we a bit testy today? Probably has to do with not getting enough sleep. I hope Miss Cardwell isn't keeping you up too late."

"I can't see how that is any of your business."

"Well, I did ensure she was provided to you. It is only good manners to enquire as to how intact she is."

"Whether she is intact or not, is still none of your business."

"Testy, testy. I would have thought you would be in a better mood after spending the night tasting her delights."

Samir gritted his teeth. A game was afoot here that he was missing. It seemed even in his own estate this man had spies. The question was, why? What could he possibly get from that? He mentally took note to review the current security arrangements with Yusef, especially any new additions to the household.

"Get to the point. Why are you calling me? Our business deal was concluded."

"It was indeed, but I thought I would do you one last favor and let you know that a team led by Grant Hamilton is in the process of breaching your walls." The voice sounded smug.

"You really should beef up your security. Any Tom, Dick, and Harry could walk straight into your little harem."

9

"What the hell does that mean?"

"Don't worry my dear Sheikh, my men are in place to help you deal with this pesky little problem." The line went dead.

Samir stood frozen looking at his phone. If the conversation he had just had meant what he thought it meant every single person on the estate was in grave danger. All he knew of his mysterious caller and benefactor was that he was a very dangerous man. His true name was unknown. He was only referred to as "The Boss" in international crime circles. Not only did he have connections everywhere but he also harbored a deep rooted hatred for the Hamilton's, even greater than the Ben Alid's. If his men had infiltrated the harem, they were at risk. He would not hesitate to gun them all down, for an opportunity to strike a blow at the Hamilton's.

Determined to stop the assault before it began, Samir brought up the number that had just called his cell, and hit redial. After three rings he heard the dreaded message "*This number has not been recognized, please try again or dial another number.*" Frantically he tried the number of the contact that had put him in touch with "The Boss"; the line was dead, as if the number had never existed.

As he stood there, momentarily frozen, he heard a noise. A soft thud against the door, followed by an almost imperceptible shuffling. Fear for his staff and concubines coursed through his veins. He dropped his cell phone, grabbed a decorative scimitar hanging on the wall and dashed to the door. Leaning against the doorframe he unlocked it slowly. With a strong push, he kicked it open and heard a thud as it hit an unknown individual behind the door. Taking a deep breath, scimitar in hand he walked straight into a war zone.

As his gaze surveyed the situation, a cold sensation spread from the pit of his stomach. His guards were engaged in hand-to-hand combat with men dressed from head to toe in black, their faces covered in masks. The fights looked macabre, like silent dances. The only noise that could be heard was grunts and fists pounding flesh. Stunned, Samir stared at the outcome of his desire for revenge. His mind racing, he remembered *Allah* (God) punished those who did wrong. He only hoped today was not the day of his punishment. Yusef and another guard rushed to his side.

"We need to get to the women," he barked to his men. Yusef nodded. Flanking him, they started moving towards the harem section of the estate. As Samir made his way through the hall, kicking and punching through the melee, one thought tormented him. He had to let Amanda go.

CHAPTER 3

Amanda woke up the next morning, lassitude sweeping through her as she thought of the night before. After the incident in the pleasure room, Samir had carried her back to his bedchambers, where they had made love two more times, before they were overtaken by sleep just before dawn.

She glanced around, and saw that Samir had left her a note. "*Habibi,*" it began, bringing a smile to her face. "Last night was memorable beyond words. Alas, my family duties fill the day, and I must leave your embrace for a few hours. I shall return by nightfall, to claim you as mine yet again. I have left instructions with Yusef and Nadia that you are to be given free reign of the estate if you so wish. Also, I have instructed that your belongings be moved out of the harem wing. I would have you sleep in my bed from now on." The note was unsigned.

As she lay on the King-size bed, clutching the message and feeling like a giddy little school girl, Amanda's thoughts drifted to the night before. It was all so crazy. The night had been a world-wind of new sensations and experiences. She had discovered a side of herself she hadn't even known she had.

When she had opened her eyes to see Samir towering over her, ready to fulfill all her sexual desires…knowing he had been watching, enjoying their performance for his pleasure. Her only thought had been *please take me*. She would have never imagined, that being forced to submit to another's sexual desires, could be so deliciously erotic and fulfilling. *No wonder I agreed to come to this harem, a place that requires total submission.*

Despite being sore from head to toe, she had to admit she was looking forward to the day to come. *A day spent in Samir's arms*. Laughing she grabbed one of the pillows and brought it to her face and inhaled. It had Samir's scent lingering on it. Rolling up in bed, still clinging to his pillow, she blinked, realizing it was well past noon. She got to her feet, her legs a bit sore and unsteady. Dressing in Samir's morning gown she made her way to the dining room, where she found another note next to a newspaper. She was flattered that she had brought out the romantic in Samir. Eager she scanned through the words:

PLEASE READ PAGE 15

Perplexed, she picked up the newspaper, to see the New York Times banner atop of the fold. It was out of date by a month or so. Since she hadn't seen a newspaper in her entire time in the estate yet, this mysterious note had her curiosity peaked. Just how was the world doing, in the weeks since she had left it to live here in paradise?

Ignoring the sports and arts section, Amanda turned to the

page suggested, which focused on the United States. Her breath caught in her throat. Staring back at her, in stark black and white, was her face, a large smile on her features. *Search For Billionaire's Kidnapped Fiancée Enters Fifth Week*, the headline screamed in bold font. Amanda read on.

"The search for Amanda Cardwell, the fiancée of billionaire, industrial tycoon Grant Hamilton, entered its fifth week today. The dramatic kidnapping has captured the attention of many in high society, not only due to the fairytale nature of their meeting, but also the almost cinematic circumstances surrounding the kidnapping..."

Amanda read the whole story twice. According to it, she had been kidnapped almost six weeks ago, after becoming engaged to Grant Hamilton. While the name tickled something in her mind, her amnesia still prevented her from placing a face to the name. The story continued by saying that after the chief suspect had been arrested, Grant had disappeared, pursuing leads with local authorities around the world trying to find his fiancée. *"Will Amanda Cardwell's fairytale romance have a fairytale ending? This newspaper writer can only pray so."*

The paper dropped to the table as Amanda stared at it numb with shock. She wanted to deny it. It had to be a joke, a bad dream. However, even as the thoughts were forming in her mind, she knew it wasn't so.

Her memories came crashing back to her. How she met Grant, how she spent the day thinking he was a groundskeeper, and still finding him irresistible. The night on the boat, his possession of her body. The engagement, and Natasha's betrayal.

Her hands started to tremble uncontrollably.

With the return of her memories came a flood of emotions.

A breathtaking *desire,* a searing *passion,* a *love* forgotten.

"Grant," she moaned, her heart aching.

Her feelings in turmoil she looked around, the opulence surrounding her suddenly appeared to be a gilded cage. She realized an inescapable truth. Her entire relationship with Samir was built on a lie. From the very beginning, the estate was a trap, made to *intoxicate, entrance,* and *seduce* her. As she played back yesterday's events, she felt violated. Their lovemaking now reduced to dirty fornication. The sense of betrayal was crippling.

The harem had once made her feel safe, made her believe she was amongst demanding but caring friends. Now she realized it was all an illusion to keep her captive. Had Odella known? Dyana? Dr. Assad? Were they all laughing at how gullible she was? Could they have been so deceitful?

Amanda walked almost catatonically to the bathroom, shedding pieces of clothing as she went. Samir's scent was still on her, clinging to her body. His very seed lingered within her.

What had once been a sign of the pleasures they had shared was now only a reminder of what a fool she had been. As she stood in the shower room, water pouring down removing all traces of his possession, she did not cry.

Once shed of all the physical reminders of her tryst, Amanda made her way to the harem wing of the estate. After entering, she drifted to her bedroom, sitting down on the mattress before placing her head in her hands. *He must have planned this all along. Why would he do this to me? What kind of sick, twisted person kidnaps someone and…and rapes them?*

Even as the thought popped into her head, Amanda knew she was in denial. Samir hadn't raped her, he had made love to her, *seduced* her mind, *conquered* her body. That was the worst betrayal of all. The feelings and memories from last night would forever be with her, reminding her, tormenting her. The very thought of what they had done, and the pleasure she had derived from it, made her feel dirty.

As tears burned behind her eyelids Amanda looked around lost, her mind unable to provide the solace she needed.

CHAPTER 4

She was a prisoner. Her mind repeated the words again, and again, refusing stoutly to give her respite from this undeniable truth. Curled in a fetal position Amanda tried to blank out her inner voice. She needed to think of something, anything beside the fact that she had fucked her jailer and had enjoyed it. *What am I going to do?*

A knock on the door interrupted her dark thoughts. "Amanda?"

She looked up to see a woman she had never seen before in her door entrance. She was tall, nearly six feet, with voluptuous curves. Her piercing blue eyes and raven's wing black hair gave her an exotic look. She could see lean muscle in the woman's thighs and arms. For some reason, she did not look like she was one of Samir's concubines.

"I'm sorry, do I know you?"

The strange woman looked over her shoulder before stepping inside. She came over and sat next to Amanda, her voice dropping to a harsh whisper. "No. But I must speak to you urgently."

"I'd rather not," Amanda said looking at her with suspicion. "Unless you have some Godiva chocolate with you and a bottle of sparkling wine, please go away."

"Sparkling wine?"

"Yes, to drown my sorrows in." It was clear this woman wasn't much for subtleties.

"Unfortunately I do not. Grant Hamilton sent me."

"Grant? You know Grant?"

The woman nodded. "My name is Tatianna Romanovsky Hamilton. I am the one who left you that note. I'm here to get you out of here."

"I...I don't think I can leave just yet." Amanda blurted out, completely startled by her own words.

"I did not know that you were enjoying this spa visit that much," Tatianna replied sarcastically. Amanda felt the heat of an unwelcome blush creeping up her cheeks. She had to admit, she had sounded less than enthusiastic.

She sat back, embarrassed. "Listen, I don't know who you are and I just found out who I am. So just give me a minute to process."

"Well, who did you think you were?" Tatianna replied curiously.

"Someone, else," Amanda snapped, "I've been suffering from retrograde amnesia."

"I see."

"I seriously doubt you do."

Tati looked at her with a penetrating gaze before responding. "You look healthy, so you haven't been beaten or starved. You have your own room with no additional guards, so you have been treated like a guest. Your rosy lips indicate you have been recently kissed, continuously. The love bites on your neck confirms this observation. The embarrassed blush on your cheeks completes the picture." Amanda squirmed at the stab of guilt that accompanied Tatianna's words. The Russian continued to look at her expressionlessly.

"Like I said – I see. However, your fiancée and my husband are waiting not far from here to take this estate, by force if need be. I think it would be better for all of us if we skipped the violence and just snuck out of here instead."

"I…yes you are right." Taking a deep breath Amanda decided getting out of her gilded cage was more important than her mixed emotions.

"Good. Let's go." Before any additional words were said, the door cracked open again and two armed men dressed in black, and wearing masks walked in. They looked dangerous and far from friendly.

"Amanda do you know these men?" Tatianna asked, eyes fixed on their visitors.

"No, I have never seen them before," Amanda replied, moving so she was standing behind Tati. The taller man took a step towards them.

"Ladies, don't make this harder than it needs to be," he said snickering. "Mind you, I don't know how my cock could get any harder." Their masked visitors chuckled. Tatianna swayed her hips, remaining silent.

"High class hookers, like you girls, are hard to find in the desert," the man continued. "James, lock the door."

"What for?" His companion asked, mesmerized by Tati's hip

movements.

"I think we have time to enjoy ourselves before getting to business." The attacker in front of Tati looked smug and lowered his weapon. "Isn't that the redhead, the girl the boss was looking for?"

"I think you are right, but he never did say anything about snatching her intact."

The assailant tucked his gun into his belt. "I don't think I will need this, I think my 'tool' will be enough." They both laughed as if he had said something extremely funny. The second man followed suite and tucked his weapon away as well.

"Stay behind me," Tatianna said to Amanda, without seeming the least bit stressed by the situation. Amanda obeyed without hesitation, her eyes desperately scanning the room for anything to use as a weapon. The shorter man started circling the women whistling appreciatively. He could have just gone for the gun he had set aside, but it was clear that for the moment he had forgotten about his mission and was more intent on satisfying his perverted urges.

"Ah, you are feisty little things. This will make it even more enjoyable."

The tall man made a burst towards Tati; she moved smoothly out of the way and drove her fist into his throat, effectively clotheslining him. He went down hard, his body hitting the floor in a sickening thud. This had the second man pausing.

"So, not so helpless after all. Well, let's just see how good you really are."

The man shifted his weight to the balls of his feet, eyes fixed on Tatianna. When the attack came Amanda was totally unprepared, and had to frantically scoot back to get out of the way. With wide eyes she watched the deadly dance that was taking place in front of her. Both opponents where evenly match. The henchman had superior strength, but Tatianna had speed and agility and she put it to use; expertly dodging his fists and kicks.

As the hand-to-hand combat became even more intense Amanda looked frantically around for anything she could use to help. That's when she spotted the gun, still tucked away in the first assailants pants. As she picked it up, she aimed at the attacker and got a shot off that shattered a vase. The room went silent.

"Hands up. Or the next bullet will be in your head."

"You don't want to be playing with toys you don't know how to use little girl," the man replied threatening, and started moving towards her.

"Listen asshole, I've had a very bad couple of months. I am NOT IN THE MOOD!" she shouted. He stopped dead in his tracks. "Hands up or I WILL shoot you. Who knows, with any luck I will miss and shoot your balls off instead?" Amanda was shaking uncontrollably.

"You don't look too experienced with that gun, little lady."

Tati walked up to Amanda and took the gun away from her. She cocked it and pointed it at the assailant. "Well I can promise you I certainly know how to shoot. On your knees."

CHAPTER 5

The next minutes were some of the longest of Amanda's life. They had quickly tied up their would-be-attackers but now came the challenge of making it out unseen. Unlocking the door, both women tried to act inconspicuous, keeping their veils over their faces and trying to act unassuming. They didn't get very far though before they bumped into Nadia. Accurately assessing her as a threat Tatianna quickly assumed a fighting stance, when Nadia held up her hands. "Peace Amazon, I am not here to stop you." She moved swiftly into an alcove, beckoning them to follow her.

"Nadia, what is going on?" Amanda asked anxiously, reassured despite herself to see a familiar foe.

Nadia turned towards her and whispered. "Keep your voice down. If you draw attention to us, even I cannot stop these invaders from finding you."

"How do you know they are not here to rescue me?"

"No man would send mercenaries to rescue his fiancée in this fashion. Not if he valued her," Nadia replied with an ironic smile. "Furthermore these sons of pigs are disrobing all the girls in search of you. That is when they're not making lewd remarks and threatening rape." As Amanda looked around she finally noticed that women where hurriedly dashing through the quarters.

"But we are not without means to protect ourselves. We have already dealt with a couple of them." Nadia pointed to four women who were trying to drag the lifeless bodies of two men into a corner.

Worry momentarily creased Nadia's brow. "The danger is very real though. For these pigs to have reached our sanctuary they must have disabled or killed the guards." Shaking her head at the thought of it she continued, "We are prepared though."

She ushered them down a small hallway. "Despite being as delicate as flowers, the women in the middle-east were bloomed in the desert, so we are as hardy and as deadly as the Sahara itself. We intend to show these men what a mistake they have made." As Amanda glanced at the bevy of beauties rushing through the hallway she realized that cleverly concealed by veils, in the palm of their hands or skirts were weapon of all sorts, knives, forks, hairpins.

Nadia strode without hesitation to a locked cabinet. "Since it is you they are after, the safest thing for the girls would be if you left, Amanda Cardwell. This is kept for the few times Samir has desired to take any of the harem girls with him overseas," Nadia explained, handing Tati and Amanda jeans and t-shirts. "I apologize if the sizes are not correct."

"It is fine," Amanda replied, pulling her top over her large breasts.

"I will stand as a look out."

After getting dressed, the two women waited, until Nadia came back. "The way is clear. I wish you both luck," Nadia said, embracing Amanda abruptly. "I hope you do not think ill of me."

"I...I don't. Thank you for helping me." Nadia nodded.

"I wish you Godspeed. Now, run swiftly down this corridor, the second door has a fake candle holder, pull it. It is a concealed door. A secret tunnel for the Masters nightly visits. At the intersection of the tunnel, take a right to navigate your way towards the fleet of vehicles. The exit is just a stone's throw away from the garage.

Hurrying through the halls, Tati kept them both at a swift pace. "When I get back to the States, promise me you're going to make sure I start doing my workouts again," Amanda huffed. As they emerged from the tunnel the women were momentarily blinded, their relief at being out quickly dissipating as two masked men materialized like genies to block their entry into the garage hanger.

"This is becoming a very energetic day," Tatianna commented drily.

"Energetic? Eh, I guess you could say that. I was going to go with shitty, crappy, and disastrous," Amanda replied without missing a beat.

Gunfire sounded in the far distance but both women focused on the men about to pounce on them. However, before anything else went down both men were struck from behind.

As they crumbled to the ground, Amanda's breath left her lungs in a long rush. She went very still, every muscle locked, frozen. There he was, her shadow man, *Grant Hamilton*.

How could she have forgotten how handsome he was? Her memories of him crystalized in an intense wave that staggered her. She almost ran to him. But she was assaulted by memories of Samir's lovemaking crashing in on an ocean of guilt. Instead she gazed at him in despair. Shuffling her feet she let her eyes stray and noticed he was standing next to a man who bore a family resemblance. She could only assume this was Alexander Hamilton. As the men stepped up to them, Amanda bit her lip until it was throbbing in tandem with her pulse.

"Hi Amanda," Grant said hesitantly.

"Hi…" she replied eyes staring at her feet. As he reached out and caressed the tendril of her hair that had fallen in front of her face, her heart did a summersault.

"I am sorry it took so long to come and get you." His words were delivered in a soft whisper.

"That's ok. Thank you for coming." Unable to resist his towering presence, with a sob, she walked into his arms.

***

Alexander watched his brother's reunion, pleased the mission looked to be a success. But as he looked around, he was very much aware they were still in enemy territory and not out of the woods yet. Keen to give his brother a few seconds of privacy he walked up to his wife marveling at how she could still take his breath away. "Hi darling, did you miss me?" he asked, before kissing her thoroughly. Smiling she whispered back, "Yes."

Alex turned to his brother, who was still holding his fiancée. "Ok boys and girls we need to get out of here stat."

His wife nodded. "Let's split up. This way they will have to track more than one target, this will undermine their efforts."

"Good idea," Alex replied turning towards his brother. "Grant here are the coordinates for our rendezvous point. The extraction is in 39hrs from now. Stay off any mobile communication devices, as these might have been compromised."

We are exiting the compound in two black jeeps. Give us some cover, Alex radioed the rescue team.

"No one is leaving here without my permission," said a calm voice. Sheikh Samir Ben Alid, Yusef, and two other guards emerged from the secret tunnel.

As Grant's eye settled on his one-time schoolmate the rage he had been containing burst. He took up a sprint and without slowing down he plowed into Samir. They both went down hard, Grant aiming a kick at Samir's face.

As they rolled, kicking and punching, Samir got the upper hand with a well-aimed kick in the stomach. As Grant propelled backwards, grunting, they both eyed each other viciously before getting up and circling around one another. Samir feigned a right punch only to swing around with a roundhouse kick. Grant blocked and delivered a punch straight into Samir's face. He then ducked under his raised fists and delivered three consecutive blows under his ribcage.

Samir's guards joined the fight, but they soon found themselves having to face off against Tatianna and Alexander Hamilton. The fighting started in earnest.

Amanda didn't know what to do. She stood in the eye of the storm, violence erupting all around her. Her heart was thumping, strained beyond endurance. She hadn't had any time to process all the things that had happened. This confrontation with Samir was too soon. As Grant finally got the upper hand and pointed a gun at Samir, she found her voice.

"STOP!" she screamed at the top of her lungs. Everyone stilled. Without any hesitation, eyes staring firmly at Samir, she started walking towards him. As Grant tried to hold her back she shook off his hand, and didn't slow down. She could feel a single hot tear run down her cheek.

"*Habibi*, I never meant to make you—"

Smack!

The slap, delivered so precisely, rang like a bell in the hanger. The silence that followed it was deafening.

"We are leaving." Without another word she turned around and walked back to Grant.

Sir we had the assailants pinned down but they are now on the move towards your position. The radioed message echoed.

"Come on Grant. That's our queue, we've gotta go." Grant was breathless with rage. The desire to finish Samir off, was gnawing at him. But as he looked at Amanda's crestfallen face, he knew this was not the time or the place. Reluctantly he lowered his gun.

"Samir, rest assured this isn't over yet. We will settle this soon." His voice laced with menace.

"*Inshallah* (if God wills it)," Samir answered.

"Don't worry, he does," replied Grant.

Gunfire started to increase outside, prompting both couples to jump into the nearest parked jeeps.

"We will see you at the rendezvous point. Don't be late." With those final words, Alex sped away, Grant hot on his tail.

As they drove off the grounds Amanda looked back, and could see Samir, staring at them his hands clenched at his side.

Her heart clenched. Unflinching she kept her eyes on him until they were out of view. She sighed deeply and longed for the days when her biggest problem was a two-timing, married cheat.

***

The roar in Grant's head refused to quiet down. He had noticed how well she looked. However, more importantly, he had noticed how her gaze had lingered on that bastard Samir. That simple gesture laid a dagger of ice into his heart.

However, now was not the time to untangle his mixed emotions, they were still in danger. Veering west, away from the estate he watched as his brother veered east. Using years of hard-won discipline, he took deep breaths until all that was left in his mind was the need to get to their escape point intact.

As they sped away, all that could be seen along the road was mile after mile of desolate desert. Flashing by on either side of the road where sparse patches of scorched scrub, prickly pear cactus, and the occasional, sorry-looking *retama* flower. The wind tore through the vast expanse, sweeping sand along the ground. Grant looked in his rear view mirror and saw a black SUV was approaching at breakneck speed. They were being pursued.

"Shit!" The word came out involuntarily.

"What is it?" Amanda queried

"We've got company." Grant's forehead wrinkled in concern.

"These can't be Samir's men," Amanda exclaimed, turning back in her seat to get a better look.

"Most likely not. Do you know what these guys are after and why they are pursuing us?"

"I know they are after me, as to why, I haven't got a clue."

Grant pressed down on the accelerator.

"They are gaining on us!" Amanda shouted, holding on for dear life. The SUV quickly caught up to them. Two menacing thugs, dressed like the other men that had attacked the estate, were inside.

"I can see that," muttered Grant. The SUV drove into the back of the jeep, jarring them both.

Grant knew the longer they stuck to the road the quicker they would be overrun. However, their pursuers SUV wouldn't fare so well across the sandy dunes of the Sahara, at least not as well as the Jeep Wrangler he was driving. "Hang on to your seat. This ride is about to get even bumpier." He shifted gears and tried to pull away from their pursuers.

One of the thugs leaned out of the passenger side window with a handgun that had a silencer attached to it. Looking decidedly smug, he started target practicing on the jeep. The first shot went high, missing the 4x4 by a couple of inches. The mercenary readjusted his grip, aimed and shot towards the jeep again. The sharp shards of the interior mirror shattering missed Grant's face by a centimeter as the bullet went through the windshield. Grant tried again to pull away from the SUV, but their pursuers were sticking close, trying to push their car off the road. Now almost side-by-side, the SUV slammed into the side of the Jeep. As he maneuvered away, Grant struggled to retain control. The two vehicles were fast approaching a bend in the road. Grant did not remove his foot from the accelerator…

"Grant, we are approaching a curve!"

"I know, hold on."

As the SUV and jeep sped down the middle of the road,

approaching the pin curve Grant suddenly slammed the jeep into the side of the other car. As the vehicles approached the turn at the last second he pulled the handbrake so the vehicle did a 180° spin. The maneuver nearly tipped the car over. The SUV, unprepared for the move, in its haste to get out of the way swerved into the uneven desert terrain and was violently flipped into the air. Without a glance back to see what happened to their assailants Grant drove the jeep off the road and into the desert at high speed.

Soon the sparse desert landscape turned into soft sand and they were driving amongst the sand dunes. Grant struggled to ensure the vehicle went up the sand dunes, but the 4x4 drifted sideways as if they were on a boat. The sensation was disorientating.

The dunes were fragile and soft, and initially the jeep just veered through them. However half an hour into their drive the car started sputtering.

"What's wrong?" Amanda asked anxiously. The sputtering suddenly ceased and the vehicle started to slow down.

As Grant checked the cars dials, he couldn't believe their bad luck. "We are out of gas. I think one of the bullets shot a hole in our tank."

They were stranded in the middle of the desert.

CHAPTER 6

Amanda watched quietly as Grant unbuckled himself and started rummaging through the jeep.

"What are you looking for?"

"Provisions. This car was parked not far from the garage entrance, it could well have been provisioned for a short trip." As he searched through the car, Grant reemerged with a smile.

"Bingo, two small bottles of water, a blanket and a couple of chocolate bars."

"That doesn't sound like a treasure to me."

"You'll change your mind once you've been out in the desert for a while." He reached inside his pocket and took out a map and a compass. Using the inbuilt GPS in the car he jotted down their location and then proceeded to smash the device.

Turning to Amanda he said, "Let's go."

"Go where? We are in the middle of the desert," she reminded him.

"We can't stay here. Notwithstanding the fact that those

goons will likely come back once they have a better equipped vehicle, this water will not last us in midday desert temperatures. We might very well die from dehydration before they ever get to us."

"But go where?"

"To our meeting point. It is only a couple of miles away. Use your veil as a head band to protect against heat stroke. If the heat doesn't kill you in the desert during the day, the cold at night will. This is why we need to go right now, to make enough headway."

"Were you a desert Bedouin in a previous life?" Amanda asked, eyebrow raised.

"Nope, but I did come out top of my class in the Boy Scouts," Grant relied with a reassuring smile.

They started their trek under the sunset, the silence between them was decidedly uncomfortable. As Grant watched Amanda through the corner of his eye, the need to ask her if she had been hurt gnawed at him. His brief glimpse of her curvy body in her harem getup seemed to imply no visible physical damage. But what had happened between her and Samir?

"Did he hurt you?" The words were blurted out without any finesse. The silence that followed was deafening. Amanda closed her eyes, desperately wishing she could take back the events of the last couple of weeks.

"No, not physically he didn't."

"So he didn't rape you?"

"No."

Grant's relief was immediate, but as he gazed intently at Amanda he realized there was something else she was holding back. He remembered the romantic pictures he had seen of her and Samir. Finally, he asked the question that had secretly been plaguing his mind, "Did you sleep with him?"

Amanda did not know what to say. There was no way she could answer this question without hurting Grant. As the sun disappeared at the horizon, she knew the only way was to be truthful. "Until Tatianna Hamilton burst into my room earlier today I didn't know who I was. I didn't know who you were or that I had been kidnapped. I thought I was there of my own free will."

Grant's gut knotted. He could hear the thud of his heart pounding in his ears, like the roar of a wounded animal.

"What are you trying to say?"

"Yes, I slept with him."

Her admission triggered something vicious and dark in him. He turned away from her and walked away. His hands clenched into tight fists, and his heart summersaulting erratically.

Amanda ached as she watched his retreating back. Samir's betrayal still stung like an open wound. Although he had coaxed her consent, the truth of their relationship had her feeling emotionally violated.

She didn't feel clean anymore. She wasn't surprised Grant walked away. She wanted to walk away from herself. Based on the ridged set of his shoulders she knew he was angry. Feeling like an abandoned puppy she wrapped her arms around herself and started walking after him.

By the time night set, the desert was a cold, barren place. Grant had been acting as if she was leper all evening. Keeping conversations to short, curt responses and waking as far ahead as possible.

They were both visibly exhausted. Amanda's mouth was as

dry as parchment despite taking small sips of water from her bottle throughout the day.

"Let's camp here for the night." These were the first words to come out of Grant's mouth voluntarily. Looking around warily, all Amanda could see apart from sand, was a large, desert rock. But as exhausted and dehydrated as she was, she didn't care where they stopped as long as they stopped. As she was about to go lie down on the other side of the rock Grant grabbed her hand.

"No. The sun rises in the east. We need to sleep west of the rock to be in the morning shade." With no further conversation he pulled her down next to him, covered them both with the blanket and went to sleep. Amanda was awake for what felt like an eternity. The warmth of Grant's body sent a rush of electricity sparkling across her skin. She didn't understand how she could have forgotten this. The mere scent of him had her squirming. *Stupid girl. You will probably die in this desert. Stop thinking about sex.* Safe in his embrace, she finally fell asleep.

***

The desert lay still under the morning sunrise, the lazy swirling of a distant dust devil the only movement to be seen. Grant was awake. He had been for hours. Taking a deep breath, he turned around and finally looked at the woman he had come to save.

His golden gaze devoured her face, taking in every shadow, noting how dry her lush lips had become. It was clear they needed to get out of this desert, the quicker the better. Determined, they would not die a million miles from home, he turned towards Amanda.

"Wake up. We need to leave, very soon." While Amanda shook the sleep from her eyes, Grant checked his compass. When they had broken down, the car's GPS app had estimated that they had another 25 miles to go before they reached the rendezvous point. At the rate they were moving, factoring in the fact they could not travel at high noon and would likely have to zigzag through mountainous, sand dunes, they had another day's worth of walking ahead of them.

***

20 Miles later

"Is this it? Have we reached the rendezvous point?"

"Yes it is just past this ridge."

Amanda nodded. Her clothes were in taters, her mouth as dry as parchment. If it hadn't been for Grant's encouragement during their trek through the hot, furnace desert she would have given up a long time ago.

If she could have, she would have cried out of relief, but she was too dehydrated to do even that. As they reached the pinnacle of the ridge they could see the rescue helicopter waiting for them.

"Come on," Grant shouted grabbing her hand. They started to run towards the helicopter. A tall man, with broad shoulders, sandy brown hair, dark brown eyes flecked with lighter specks, and a carbine machine gun in his hands, stepped out of the side door of the UH-60. "Mr. and Mrs. Hamilton," he shouted.

"Yes, we are the Hamiltons!" Grant shouted back.

"We are your ride home," the pilot yelled. "This area isn't secure we need to get airborne as quickly as possible!"

Grant nodded, and guided Amanda into the waiting chopper. Helping her in, he strapped her into a jumpseat in the back.

"Where are my brother and his wife?"

"They are waiting for you at basecamp. Mr. Hamilton sustained a flesh wound during the initial escape."

As soon as they were belted in, the pilot pulled back on the control stick, and the chopper shot into the air, banking quickly before heading out towards the ocean.

An armed guard sat at the entrance of the chopper, manning a mounted machine gun. As the chopper blades whined overhead taking them to safety, Amanda wondered if things were ever going to be the same again.

CHAPTER 7

2 weeks later Hamptons, New York

A lexander Hamilton stood next to his brother, reaching for the remote control in his hand. "Jesus Grant, do you really need to keep torturing yourself?"

Grant snatched his arm away, giving his brother a withering stare. "I need to know, Alex. Just how far it went."

"For fuck's sake, she had amnesia! She barely remembered her name the whole time. Combine that with physical stress, emotional displacement, and a bunch of other things that let's just say the CIA taught me more about than I ever wanted to know in my life, and yes, things probably got a bit steamy between them."

Grant ignored his brother, and turned his attention back to the video monitor. He clicked the play button on the remote, and watched as Samir tweaked Amanda's nipple through her silken harem top. She leaned back, her legs spreading in want. The bastard continued to nibble and suck at her neck, before he reached between her legs. She pushed away, kicking at him, before what looked like tears came to her eyes and she stumbled, falling to the floor. The scene continued, but Grant turned away, his emotions in turmoil.

It had been two weeks since Amanda's rescue. Every time he looked at her, he felt like his heart had been ripped from his chest. Shame and anger were waging a war within him. Shame, that he let her be taken. Anger, that there might have been something more than a jailer/kidnapper relationship between her and Samir. He was plagued with thoughts that she actually cared for him. And that shamed him more than else.

What if she wished she were still back with him? The lost look in her eyes every time they were together made him blaze with futile rage. He knew the logic of it, she was innocent, but his bruised heart was aching at the images he was seeing.

He didn't know what to do with his anger. Never mind how much he denied it out loud he WAS angry at her, but he was even angrier at himself and at Samir. Fuck! He was angry at the whole damned world and he didn't know how to stop.

"Why has Samir got it in for you like a bad rash?" Alexander asked. "I can only imagine he is the one who sent you this tape."

"The package was anonymous, but who else? He probably orchestrated the kidnapping because of what happened with Amirah." Grant replied, his eyes cold as icicles.

"His sister? Why'd you dump her, anyway?" Alexander asked, looking bewildered. "You didn't go about it in the most subtle of way. What did she do?"

Grant ran a hand through his hair, breathing shakily as he

struggled to control his emotions. "She didn't do anything wrong. It's just that.... well.... she wasn't my type."

"When you dumped her, you shamed the eldest daughter of a Muslim Middle Eastern oil baron. Jesus Grant, that was some stupid shit," Alex said, "You fucked a virgin, the eldest sister of one of your rivals, and let her go. I'm surprised this didn't bite you in the ass years ago." Grant didn't bother responding.

"Did you hurt her?" Alex asked softly.

"No, dammit!" Grant retorted vehemently, spinning to face his brother. Trying to calm down he took a deep breath and responded, "The irony is I never touched her."

"What?" Alex almost choked on his gin and tonic.

"You heard me, I didn't touch her. Amirah and I were dating platonically for a couple of weeks, but we both knew it wasn't going anywhere. One night I found her disheveled and sobbing on the estate grounds. She had been sleeping with some millionaire shit-head who after taking her virginity that very night had dumped her. I promised never to tell. Everyone just assumed since the two of us were dating, I was the culprit in the story. Samir was always a patient, vindictive man," Grant explained, a muscle flicking angrily at his jaw. "Listen Alex, I know I got lucky. And I'm thankful for your help as well as Tati's. But this is out of your hands now. Clearly the sick S.O.B is playing some twisted game."

"Twisted is a mild way of putting it. Does Amanda know you have this tape?"

"No, and I want to keep it that way. Now don't you have a bombshell of a wife to get back to?"

Alexander came over and gave his brother a hug, slapping him on the back. "Hang in there big brother. I am sure between

Chase and Jake's efforts you will nail the bastard where it hurts."

Grant returned the hug. "Thanks, Alex. Now, get out of here before I throw you out."

Alexander let go of his brother, looking him in the eye. "Just promise me you'll talk to me before you think of doing anything else completely stupid, okay?"

"Sure, I will stick to only slightly stupid."

Grant grimaced, and Alexander shook his head and left. As soon as Grant was alone in his library, he hit the play button again. Outside, the moon over the Gulf of Mexico set, and the night birds cried out in the Florida darkness.

***

"Emma, I don't know what to do." Desperate for advice Amanda had locked herself in the study with her favorite gadget, the iPhone. She was having a face-to-face conference with Emma Baker, her best friend.

"I thought you guys had sorted it by now. According to the media you had some kind of daring rescue and your fairytale wedding was back on."

"The media announcement and photo-shoots were just for show. We haven't been intimate since I got back."

"What do you mean you haven't been intimate? Not even a peck on the cheek?"

"No."

"Hand holding?"

"No."

"Does he know about you and Samir?"

"I told him we slept together."

"Damn, you are in deep shit."

"Yep that's me. Up shit creek without a paddle," Amanda replied as she curled up on the sofa in the study. Despite her spunky words she felt bereft and alone. Everything was so different now between her and Grant.

"What were you thinking? A man will forgive anything, but after frantically looking for you all over the world, finding out you are playing lovers with your kidnapper is probably not one of them."

"Ems you know it wasn't like that. It has taken me the last couple of weeks to stop wanting to wring Samir's neck," Amanda replied with a sigh. What she didn't want to admit, even to her best friend was how she still felt dirty and now so unworthy of Grant's love. She had a hard enough time admitting it to herself.

"So we can conclude you are not in love with tall, dark, and dangerous then?"

"I can't believe you even bothered stating the *blatantly obvious*. What happened with Samir was way worse than Scott, the two-timing bastard. At least with Scott, it was my decision, *me, Amanda*, not some amnesic girl scammed into a sexual romp. I might have been confused right after I found out, but I'm over it."

"Calm down, I was just asking, jeez."

"Ems, I just want Grant back, and I don't know what to do so he wants to be with me again," Amanda replied in a tear-smothered voice.

"Calm down. You are just going to have to do anything and everything."

"What do you mean?"

"Amanda, do you know the lengths Grant went to, to get you guys together? I am not just talking about rushing across the world and saving you from some sex fiend. That in itself is worth a medal, but the length he went through before you even met. I mean, he took one look at you in my summer pictures and that was it. He had to meet you. Once I showed him our crazy videos he was even more adamant. If I hadn't thought you guys would be a match made in heaven I wouldn't have gone along with his scheme to lure you to his mansion." Emma's word felt like a soothing balm over Amanda's raw nerves.

"The guy fell madly in love with you, even before meeting you. The question is this, do you love him as madly? If you do, then you need to do anything and everything to make him forget your unwanted liaison with Samir. Remind him he loves you."

"How the heck do I do that?"

"Well you could start by talking to him, instead of talking to me. Swiftly followed by a rumble in the haystack and that should get you guys back on the right track."

"Thanks Ems, I didn't know you turned into an agony aunt while I was gone?"

"You can thank me at your wedding."

CHAPTER 8

Spurred by her conversation with Emma, Amanda decided to take the bull by the horns and seek out Grant. After they returned to the estate he moved into one of the en-suite rooms located on the other side of his mansion. She had never set foot there, but tonight she would seek him out in his private refuge.

"Grant?" she whispered tentatively as she tiptoed into the suite. She made a full stop at the threshold and stared open mouthed. The room was enormous. It had a separate dining area with a side entrance to the main sleeping area. There was a mahogany, four-poster bed centered in the room and the entire wall opposite the bed was covered in a gigantic mirror.

"Grant? Are you here?" With apprehension, she walked further into his bedroom.

"What are you doing here?" At the sound of Grant's less than pleased tone Amanda whipped around and caught her breath. He stood at the entrance of the room, with only a towel around his waist, his torso still slightly damp from his shower. He looked breathtakingly handsome.

"I was just…eh. I wanted to have a chat, but since you are busy I will come back some other time."

Grant shook his head and walked over to the walk-in wardrobe. "This is as good a time as any." Completely ignoring her, he reached for a towel and started drying his hair.

"I just wanted to know if you were up for dinner tonight. Just the two of us down by the lake."

Grant tilted his head, curious. "Oh? Why?"

Amanda pondered her answer for a moment, and chose the least controversial response. "Well, I know these past weeks have been strained," she replied. "And I'm sorry for being so withdrawn. You've been a total gentleman this whole time, and I thought we could get a fresh start."

Grant stared at her silently before responding. "Amanda, I would be more than happy to start again, that said you've got to get yourself checked out first."

"Checked out?" Amanda stated, puzzled.

Grant nodded and looked away. "We should have done it as soon as you got back, but I delayed because I knew you needed some time to reacclimatize to America. But a doctor really should check you out after what you've been through. Who knows if there is any long term danger from that knock to your head, or the drugs you were injected with?" The words "*and your lovemaking to Samir*" hung silently between them.

Unable to stand the tension that was between them, Amanda blurted out, "Why don't you just get it out? I'm tired of this little game we are playing."

"Get what out?" Grant replied, his golden brown eyes staring intensely into hers.

"Whatever it is that you've been dying to say."

"Really?" Grant's reply was delivered as soft as a dangerous whisper, promising her, wherever she was taking this conversation she really didn't want to go there.

A wave of despair swept through her. She wished she could break down the walls that were keeping them apart. That he would kiss her, slip inside her, and forget the events that had separated them.

Realizing that she would have to push the subject or maybe forever lose him, Amanda took her courage in hand and pressed on. "You haven't touched me since we got back."

Her words hung between them like a silent condemnation. Grant put aside his second towel and walked towards her. He didn't stop until she was near enough to feel the heat of him. Amanda gulped.

"Touched you? You want me to touch you?" His gaze trailed along her alabaster neck, down to her creamy heaving bosom.

"Who am I to refuse? If the lady wants to be touched, touched you shall be." With no additional warning, he swung her around, pressing her back firmly against the hard length of him. There was no mistaking his desire for her. His member could have been made out of marble.

"Grant, what are you doing?" Amanda whispered, breathlessly.

"Touching you. Isn't that what you requested?" His warm breath was sending tendrils of hot desire down her spine.

"Do you want me to touch you here?" his fingers grazed her puckered nipple. "Or here?" He ground his cock against her backside. "Is that rough enough or would you like it rougher, like your Arabian lover."

At his vicious words Amanda tore herself free and turned around to face him. "He wasn't my lover by choice and you know it."

"It didn't stop you from enjoying it *darling*." And there it was, her secret shame. The wall that was between them finally crystalized.

She could not deny the pleasure that Samir had given her, and for that she was still cursing his name.

"Never mind, this conversation is pointless. I will leave you to it," Amanda retorted and started walking towards the exit. She barely took a step, before she was roughly pulled into Grant's arms again, his lips crushing hers in a bruising kiss. Although she should have been outraged, a small part of her was just relieved to feel him against her. She'd been so afraid he'd never want to touch her again.

"When he kissed your lips did he make you feel like this?" Grant muttered, as he continued his punishing exploration.

"Grant don't. Please stop. Not like this, not in anger. Please." Even as the words left her lips, her body was betraying her, her nipples straining for his attention. He lifted up her skirt and without hesitation inserted his chunky finger in her wet sheet. Amanda's legs buckled.

"When he fucked you did you juice as much as you are juicing for me?" Grant's words were laced with torment.

"Please stop," Amanda moaned.

"Did you tell HIM to stop, or were you enjoying yourself too much?" *How did you not know you were mine?*

"I...I can't change anything that happened. And I can't deny that he didn't force himself on me. But that was before – before

I knew," she whimpered.

Her words nearly shattered him. He knew what it was like to fill her, to stretch her. He knew what it was like to have her ride him, slick with hot heat, and he resented that any other man before or since him had ever made a claim on her. It was irrational, unfair but her pleading voice could not assuage his anger... his shame.

"I can't deny I wanted you from the very first moment I saw you," he whispered in her ear, while his digit continued to slowly fuck her.

"If you want to be with me, this is all I have left to offer you." He inserted a second digit into her tight tunnel and used his left hand to stroke her nipple. "*Need, hunger, possession.*" Amanda found herself juicing copiously, the muscles in her stomach starting to clench. She knew this was punishment. He was deliberately using sex against her, but her body remembered how a mere touch from him could solicit intense pleasure. As he claimed her mouth with his, she didn't have the willpower to resist; instead her fingers fisted in his hair, holding him to her. She closed her eyes and savored the feel of his tongue and the heat of his mouth as he suckled her lower lip. He wasn't gentle, his teeth scrapping against hers, but her body reacted with an urgency that had her nearly sobbing.

"Did he make you feel like this? Did you get wet for him, dammit?" his words were growled like an animal in pain. Abruptly he stepped away from her. Panting they stared at each other. His next sentence was uttered without a shred of emotion.

"Your total submission is what I *crave*. Give it to me, or get the hell out of my bedroom." His glittering eyes met hers, cold, possessive, and utterly without mercy. Her pulse began a frantic rhythm.

Amanda knew she had to make a decision. It was now or never. If she denied him they might never be able to bridge what had happened. When she closed her eyes it wasn't Samir's brown eyes she glimpsed inside her mind. It was hazel eyes, blazing with determination, Grant's eyes. She stilled. Suddenly she knew without a shadow of a doubt she would do anything to be with him. She looked at Grant and nodded as she touched her tongue to her tender lips. That was all the permission Grant needed.

Grabbing a hold of her like a drowning man to a lifeboat, he claimed her lips again, forcefully starting an erotic dance with their tongues as the main players. Amanda's body went up in flames. As he took command, one fist in her thick auburn hair, he forced her head back, his tongue dueling with hers. He plundered her mouth, and she couldn't think a coherent thought. All she knew was that she wanted more.

When he pulled away from her, she had trouble catching her breath. How she had missed this. Through just one kiss he was more addictive than any other man she had ever met or been with.

Panting Grant stared at her, determination written all over his face. "Take off your clothes and get on the bed on all fours." His voice brokered no argument. Committed she walked slowly to the bed. As she shed her clothes, she could feel the heat of his gaze burning her. Wearing only her cotton underwear, she climbed on to the bed and went on all fours.

She watched him in the mirror as he removed the towel around his hips and dropped it on the floor. He was magnificent. His cock jutting out like a sword, ready to conquer.

The sight of him had her salivating.

He walked towards a chest of drawers and emerged with a riding crop. She stared wide-eyed. What did he intend to do with that? Her racing heart doubled in pace. She was determined not to run or cry, whatever may happen, so she stayed put.

He paced up to her, the riding crop in one hand. As her eyes met his, she knew what was to come might require more than total submission. His desire was set to devour her, mind, body, and soul. She knew she welcomed it. She *needed* it.

As he got closer, Amanda shut her eyes bracing herself for what was to come. She knew he felt betrayed, but she had never thought this would be the price she had to pay.

As irrational as it was, it was her shame that kept her in place on all fours. She had a twisted desire to do penance. She needed to be cleansed in the flames of his passion, to make it right, for both of them.

Since it was clear total submission was the only penance he would accept. She was more than willing to pay, if only so that he would love her again, just a little, as he had before.

.

CHAPTER 9

Grant had never wanted a woman more than he wanted Amanda in that moment. As she lay on all fours, her bottom his to command and possess, he knew the punishment he had in store for her would inevitably torment them both and provide ultimate satisfaction.

Grant wished things could have been different. When he had first devised the plan to make her his bride, he had good intentions. He had intended to show her his gentle side. He would cage the beast that lived inside him. Cage it until they knew each other more intimately. Teach her the darker, more erotic play in increments. Make her slowly understand his need for sexual control.

For a while, he had thought it would work. Then Samir had taken her. Taken what was his. His need for her total submission now blazed like an inferno. The only way to quench the fire was to let it burn.

Although his conscience was screaming to him to stop the

path he was on, she was a weakness he was not man enough to walk away from. He was going to show her who she belonged with. Make her yearn and ache. Make her crave his touch and ruin her for everyone else *forever*. She was his and he intended to make sure she knew it. If he could, he would have claimed her very soul. Instead, he intended to possess her in a way Samir never had. *Completely.*

Grant crawled onto the bed, sitting down on his knees between Amanda's legs. He didn't touch her, just trailed the leather tip of the riding crop over the expanse of her creamy thighs.

Amanda's heart began beating frantically. Her eyes widened as he opened up the lips of her labia, eased through the folds, scooping up her creamy wetness and spreading it delicately around her entrance. The pleasure was instantaneous and intense. She closed her eyes and moaned.

"Look at me, look at what I am doing to you," he whispered tersely in her ear. She opened her eyes and looked. The image was beyond erotic. She looked wanton. She should have been ashamed but she wasn't. She wanted this man with every fiber of her being.

He grabbed a hold of her panties and pulled them to the side. The thought of what he was looking at, had her blushing. Eyes riveted to the mirror she watched him devour her womanhood with his gaze. Amanda swallowed hard.

Gazing at her hotly, Grant unhooked her bra, and her big creamy breasts bounced free. "My cock has hungered for only you over the last couple of months. It won't hunger for anyone else anymore." His hand still holding her briefs pulled to the side, he took his member in his other hand and positioned it at her entrance. "As only your body will do, your body is mine." That was all the preparation she had. Not bothering to pull her panties off, he moved, ramming her hard, balls deep. Amanda gasped at the delicious intrusion, her tight channel stretching achingly to accommodate all of him. Her eyes glazed over with feverish need.

"From now on you are mine baby doll. Mine to fuck whenever and however I want," Grant whispered in her ear. He moved back and rammed his cock into her again, hard. Her stomach muscles clenched. "I will spread your legs every morning and deposit my seed deep inside you." She sobbed as he drove his stiff member so deep into her she thought he would fuse them together. Her desire for his possession spurred her to spread her legs even wider.

"There isn't an inch of your body I won't know intimately. My needs are yours to satisfy, as yours are mine. And satisfy them I will." His strong hands held her hips still so she could only submit to receiving his deep invasion. The coil in her stomach tightened.

He pumped his shaft hard into her tunnel. Her juices flowed liberally, soaking the underwear she was still wearing. She wondered how she could ever have thought anyone else could ever compare. It was heavenly. His complete possession of her, made her want to weep with joy, despite the anger that spurred it.

He rode her. Hard. Relentlessly.

"What's my name?" he asked pumping his cock as deep as he could.

"Grant," she groaned.

"And who do you want?" He was now fucking her so

thoroughly; his head was pounding her womb. She did not stop juicing.

"Grant, Grant, Grant." She chanted, in a pleading voice that threatened to shatter what was left of his self-control. He pumped into her hard, one last time and simultaneously pinched her clit. Her stomach muscles tightened, and she lost control. Her orgasm swept through her like a tidal wave. As her muscles clenched around his cock Grant almost came. He pulled his jutting tool out of her before the sensations overcame him.

"I am not done with you yet," he muttered. Before she could register what was happening, he grabbed her panties and tore them off her. As he buried his face in her briefs, sniffing the aroma of her come, he muttered gutturally, "You won't be needing this for the rest of the evening baby doll." Amanda's face flushed red and she buried her face quickly in the mattress, too embarrassed to watch.

"It's your sweetness that makes me want to possess you," he whispered as he caressed the back of her head. "Now, spread your legs for me." Amanda gulped, but with her eyes closed did as she was told.

Practiced fingers started swirling around her nub, teasing it with an expert rhythm. It wasn't in the speed. It was in the slightest shift, the way he knew how to arouse her. She groaned. Then the fingers were just gone and a swift, short sting on her clit startled her.

"You didn't think this whip was just for show did you?"

Amanda opened her eyes and looked at the mirror wall. Her panties were now in shreds on the floor and Grant was using the crop, with expert flicks to tap on her pussy. It wasn't hard, not enough to cause her intense pain, but still bites, little bites of pounding against her nub in a completely different way. The pain/pleasure of it was exquisite.

Grant alternated between the crop and his fingers for what felt like forever, until the juices of her wet pussy had stained the bed. Then he stopped.

"Turn around," he commanded. As she lay displayed in front of him, his gaze raked over her naked body and Amanda knew he liked what he saw. Her stomach tightened. He went down between her legs. His finger trailed over her swollen nub and lips, she moaned, desire flowing like molten lava.

"Yes, I think you are almost tender enough. Your lips down here are so beautifully puffy, baby doll." Suddenly he bent over, lifted her legs over her head and licked her swollen mound. She almost flew off the bed. Immobilizing her with one hand he continued to eat her copious juices, as she writhed on the bed. Unable to restrain herself Amanda mewled like a cat and came apart. She convulsed repeatedly as Grant swallowed her delicious creaminess. Spent, she lay limbless on the bed.

Grant's pulse was thudding in his ears, his control on a shoestring. He grabbed a hold of his erection and started massaging it against Amanda's entrance. Exhausted from overstimulation she moaned softly at the intrusion. She hissed in surprise at the girth of his tip as it founds its way between her puffy folds, reaching her achy crevice.

"Your tender pussy feels so good," he muttered. He lubricated his shaft by dipping it in and out of her hot cleft, trembling in his effort to restrain his desire. Her legs over her head, was giving him a heart stopping view of her rear passage. "Your backside is perfection," he grunted. He kneaded her peachy rear – then proceeded to brush a finger between her cheeks. Amanda groaned in protest, still in the grips of her aftermath.

"Shhh," he whispered soothingly, his voice a velvet murmur. His finger didn't stop for an instant caressing her secret entrance. "Have you ever had a man take you back here baby doll?"

"No," she answered, stains of scarlet appearing on her cheeks.

"Good," he replied, swirling his finger around her knob, then along her pussy lips all the way to her rear passage again. The thought of fucking her there, taking her so completely, made his cock impossibly harder. "It would please me enormously to possess you there. I want to be your first and your last."

Amanda hissed at his admission, at his naked need. Her heart turned over.

"You do want to please me, don't you?"

"Yes." Her whispered confession was laced with longing.

"Good girl."

He proceeded to dip into her sweet cleft, once, twice, the third time he pushed his hard erection gently into her puckered opening. She stilled. Slowly, he rubbed the tip of his shaft against her rear entrance. He returned his hand to her ass cheeks, spreading them widely. Then he pushed his shaft in, one delicious inch at a time. Amanda moaned at the intrusion.

Unrelenting, he pushed harder until finally with a satisfying plop, her anal muscles swallowed the head of his cock and gripped it like a vice.

He trembled as they both remained still, his member throbbing inside her. Her back passage was deliciously hot. The position he had her in meant she was wide open to him, unable to deny him this rare treat, even if she now wanted to. His pelvis rubbed against her engorged clit as he slid further in, headless of the tremor that touched her rosy lips.

Unwilling to deny her desperate desire for his possession, Amanda gritted her teeth against the pain and pushed upwards in an effort to take him even deeper. As the entire length of his hard cock finally pushed through her sphincter and settled firmly in her rear, she revelled in the knowledge she had finally done it, given him every part of her.

As he started administering delicious punishment with his tool, she was soon moaning, incoherently, tearfully, "I am sorry." *Please want me.*

He pulled out of her almost completely, and thrust back in mercilessly. He was opening her up in ways she had never imagined. Her sobs grew in strength. Her pleas an inarticulate prayer, "I will be good." *Please love me.*

His rhythmic pumping only increased in intensity. The pain of his intrusion was delicious; it flowed over her like a healing balm, mingling devilishly with her desire for his full and complete possession. His cock was pumping in and out of her rear balls deep. With each slow, rhythmic motion, she felt cleansed, her body welcoming his ownership. She gave a groan of pain, satisfaction, and pleasure, her anal and stomach muscles tightening in tandem.

Watching her tear up, a secret, dark part of Grant became even more aroused at the dark play she was willing to endure for his pleasure. He could not deny the sweet ecstasy of her submission…he could not…deny his love for her.

He leaned over, his cock deep in her ass and kissed his replacement, mail-order bride passionately. Gutturally he whispered, "You are a *good* girl. You are *my* girl." As he pumped her rear passage, his tongue savored her. Each movement was slow, deliberate, and precise, all with the intention of possessing every inch of her. All with the intention of saying, "I love you. I need you." The harder and deeper he pumped, the longer and sweeter he kissed her.

"I tried to save you," he muttered. "Save you from this beast that lives inside me. The one that wants to devour you. You should have left when you could." He was fucking her ass like a madman. "Now it's too late," he groaned. His cock pounded in and out of her relentlessly, bringing them both to a fever pitch. Then he slipped his hand between her legs and slightly pinched her swollen nub. Amanda's orgasm ripped through her like a tornado, her anal passage spasming around his cock.

Unable to restrain himself any longer, Grant screamed long and hard as he unleashed his seed deep inside her. His orgasm rocked him from head to toe. Exhausted he collapsed on top of her, his cock still twitching, squirting the last load of sperm into her tight passage. Panting, Grant basked in the glow of the greatest sexual experience of his life. He pulled up the blanket and gathered her in his arms.

"I love you Amanda. You are the very air that I breathe and I will never let you go."

More fulfilled than she had ever been in her life, Amanda clung to him, smiling blissfully as she fell asleep.

.

EPILOGUE

Grant Hamilton was at his wedding reception. More accurately, he was in his home office. As he looked at the desktop picture of his beautiful wife, he marveled at the fact, they were now bound together forever. Ever since that night, when Amanda had shown him how far she was willing to go for their love, how completely she was prepared to surrender to him…he had found peace. There was an unspoken agreement between them, never to speak of what had happened. They had both gotten what they needed that evening, the means to heal the rift that had been created between them. He couldn't have been luckier if he tried.

He had a woman that loved him and who relished his darker pleasures. It helped that Amanda enjoyed being his sex slave between the sheets. Though, she still blushed and hid her head in the pillows whenever he tried to pleasure her orally. Little did she understand that her creaminess was like the sweetest nectar to him. Goddess and vixen all rolled into one, now all his.

Smiling to himself he turned his attention back to his visitor.

"Is it done?" he asked Jake Hamilton, eager to hear his cousin's report.

"Yes. The fake holdings we set up were a perfect trap. The Ben Alid fortune is about to take a very steep nosedive. I would be surprised if their wealth isn't all but wiped out in the next 6 months."

Grant smiled with satisfaction and shook his cousin's hand. "Thanks cuz." Revenge had been long in coming, but poverty was about to teach a very valuable lesson to Sheikh Samir Ben Alid.

"What about the other matter we discussed. Are you up for it? I know it is not quite your cup of tea."

Jake Hamilton owned a prestigious law firm in Boston. He was known as "The Shark" in legal circles. He was overqualified for grunt work, but he was also the only person Grant could count on to investigate the latest goings on at Hamilton Industries.

Asking him to go undercover at the Hamilton Industries' subsidiary had been Chase's idea. He remembered that Jake had told him how frustrated and bored he was with the types of clients they were receiving.

"Pretending to be a boring junior clerk while trying to uncover the mole at Hamilton Industries that has been selling our tech secrets to the Saudis? Not a problem," Jake replied with a smile. "I could use a break from running my own company."

"I knew I could count on you."

Laughing the cousins hugged and walk out of the meeting room.

AUTHOR NOTE

Thank you so much for reading my book. I love writing and I hope you liked reading this story as much as I liked writing it.

As you probably know, many people look at the reviews on Amazon before they decide to purchase a book. If you liked the book, **could you please take a minute** to leave a review on your local website with your feedback if you purchased this title online?

60 seconds is all I'm asking for, and it would mean the world to me.

Thank you so much,

Montana Night

HIS DESIRE FOR HER BLAZED LIKE AN INFERNO

MONTANA NIGHT
BILLIONAIRE
ROMANCE

THE STAND IN
Bride

A Hamilton Family Saga

London born Rebecca Martin has spent the last four frustrating years working in the US at CorpSec a private security company catering for the rich and famous. Today, she just got her big break. An opportunity to be wealthy owner Chase Hamilton's personal assistant.

The man is lethal, has a smile to die for and the body and face of a very wicked angel. The attraction is instant, visceral. But she knows he's just too rich, too handsome, too everything to notice the way his plump mahogany replacement secretary has the hots for him. But a case of immigration issues with as Russian mail-order bride is just about to throw her in the path of her tantalizing billionaire boss.

Can be purchased at **amazon, barnes and noble, kobo, ibookstore** and other reputable online and offline retailers.

HIS PASSIONS WOULD NOT BE DENIED

Billionaire Alexander Hamilton has hidden behind the persona of a dull, fop to deceive the world for so long he rarely shows his true self in public. But Tatiyanna Romanovsky might just be the girl to break down those walls. Ever since they locked heads, his legendary patience has been nowhere to be seen.

When Tati is almost assassinated on US soil Alexander's protective, dominant, possessive male instincts flare to life, leaving him with an intense need to protect and claim this Russian mail-order bride.

Can be purchased at **amazon, barnes and noble, kobo,** ibookstore and other reputable online and offline retailers.